ABSORBED BY EXCREMENT

MICHAEL ERROL SWAIM

Carnage House, LLC
This is Your Trigger Warning

www.carnagehouse.com

Carnage House, LLC
www.carnagehouse.com

Published in the United States of America

ACKNOWLEDGMENTS

BIG THANK YOU TO Josh Darling and Jacque Day. Josh, you got me back into writing after decades away, but you both guided me and taught me so much. I can't thank you enough for all the hard work you put into making this book happen, and for making me look better than what I am. You're the best friends a guy could ever hope for.

My dad, Frank Swaim: You probably won't read this because of the subject matter, but you always pushed me to keep writing so thank you for that.

And I can't forget those that have helped me along the way: Jerry Blaze, Aaron Lebold, Lindsey Goddard, Kasey Hill, Tim Tolbert, J. Rocky Colavito, Chris McAuley, Jeani Rector, Pixie Bruner, Mandy Swaim, Kurt Swaim, Brianna Swaim, my cat Wolfgirl, Curtis Clinton, Jasmine Clinton, Aaron Morris, Keri Morris.

And Clive Barker for showing us the way.

Finally, to my mom Rita Ann Swaim, and my uncle Byron Morris. Wish you both could see this.

If I forgot anyone please forgive me.

CHAPTER 1

M Y DAD DID THE best he could raising me after Mom died. I was nine when it happened. Car accident. It was snowing. The freshly paved road was slick. They said she swerved to avoid hitting a deer and lost control. The little Toyota she was driving slid off the road, crashed through a barbed wire fence, went down an embankment, and flipped three times before coming to rest in a field full of cows. She hit her head on the roof as the car flipped and died later at the hospital from a brain aneurysm. We made it there in time to watch her take her last breath. I remember the cuts and bruises, the giant gash stapled together from her left eye to the back of her half-shaved head.

It fucked my family up.

Grandma killed herself the next year.

Grandpa drank himself to death shortly after.

It was me and my dad after that. He tried his best. He was a great parent, but a terrible cook in my opinion, always trying to make Gordon Ramsay-level shit. Nasty. He tried to make healthy stuff, but undercooked everything it seemed like. We didn't have much money so I had to eat what he served. If I didn't, I would go hungry. He wouldn't beat me, but he'd be disappointed, and that was worse than a beating. I don't know how many bloody hamburgers and other shit like that I ate, but I survived. Dad worked hard and ensured I had everything I needed. He encouraged me to read daily. That's why I became a writer. At least, he gave me that gift. He was my biggest fan, and even if he didn't like my work, he still praised it. Life was good with Dad.

Until he murdered someone.

I'll never forget the day my life changed. July 28, twenty-five years ago. My birthday. I was finally twenty-one, and we were at Walmart shopping for beer in the old shit-brown 1986 Ford F-150 that he had given me that morning as a gift. I used to hate that truck. Now that it was mine, I loved it. Funny how shit works out like that. We had all our tackle in the truck too since we were going to celebrate by fishing and getting drunk as fuck.

We could have gone to a liquor store to get better stuff, but we had to save money. Dad was a cook who thought he was a chef, and didn't earn a whole lot, so we shopped cheap for everything. He went to get us a bag of chips and a couple of other snacks, and I made my way down the beer aisle to see what was available. My cart bumped into this bitch with fat rolls spilling out of her too-small shorts and top. She wasn't wearing a bra and her tits sagged so low I was amazed she didn't trip over them. Her hair hung in greasy strands, and zits dotted her face. Her cart was full of Doritos and bags of Reese's cups and boxes of Little Debbie snack cakes. She smelled like a cross between a septic tank and a casino.

"What the fuck?" she screamed.

"I'm sorry ma'am, I..."

"Sorry ain't good enough, moron. Why dontcha watch where yer going?"

"Lady, I barely touched you with the cart."

A skinny man with meth teeth appeared behind her. Fuck, he stank worse than she did, like he took a bath in horse piss and hot diarrhea. Once she told him what happened, he started yelling at me. I stood there and took the abuse. I knew Dad would be back soon and would handle this. He once beat a dude to a pulp in a Walgreens because the guy held my head against his ass and ripped a nasty wet fart. Pretty sure the guy shit himself when my dad broke his nose. Hilarious.

Dad came down the beer aisle and started yelling at Meth Guy and Diabetes Lady. It escalated, and the manager told them to take it outside. Dad followed those two dumb fucks while I pushed the cart through the checkout line with my birthday beer. I couldn't understand why that lady was so upset. I barely bumped her. I doubt it hurt her. It was fucking dumb. Stupid bitch.

I walked out the front door with my beer, smiling and thinking, *Finally, I'm an adult*. But my happiness was short-lived. Some dumbass cops had slammed Dad up against a police car. He was slumped over the hood, hand-cuffed and bleeding from his forehead. An officer held back Diabetes Lady. She was screaming and reaching for her husband who lay face down in a pool of his own blood. We were supposed to spend the rest of my birthday drinking and fishing.

Not anymore.

I don't know how long I stood there, watching the blood spread under Diabetes Lady's husband, mesmerized by the dying man's wound. I could see the cut across his throat and hear him gurgling through his severed trachea as he attempted to take his final breaths. His death rattle sounded deep, wet, and snotty. I don't know how else to explain it. Not long after, the body twitched, and he was dead. Most people would look away. Not me. I loved it. I had never seen anything so interesting. Kinda made my dick hard, and it calmed me. I know, weird, but it also helped shape my writing to what it is today.

When all was said and done, Dad went to prison for doing the guy in. In his rage, Dad had grabbed my filet knife out of the tackle box in the back of the truck and slit Meth Guy's throat. There was no getting around the charges. He knew it and pled guilty at the trial. People had watched him kill that guy too, so plenty of witnesses.

Since Dad was fresh meat in jail, the inmates beat the shit out of him his first night in lockup. He ended up with a broken nose, a dislocated jaw, and several fractured ribs. Bruises everywhere. I wouldn't have heard about it if not for the warden, who called to tell me Dad might not make it. He did. He survived that beating and many more. Dad was a tough old bastard. I tried to visit as much as I could. I didn't see him as a murderer. My dad was a fucking hero. He had defended me that day, as a father should, and I have never forgotten.

I am proud of him for that.

When I saw him on visiting days, he looked terrible, often with black eyes and bruises. He'd always smile for me. We discussed what was happening in my life. One day not long before his lights went out for good, I told him I had met someone. Mary was her name, and Dad was happy for me. Me and Mary were to be married the next year. He was proud.

A few weeks later, I got a call from the warden. Dad was dead. Extreme trauma to the anus, they said. A fancy way to say he got butt-fucked to death. Not a pleasant way to go. The bastards left him to die on his bunk, blood, jizz, and shit leaking out of his asshole.

It's a sad story, but that's how I found out he had ten acres of land. I didn't know he owned anything like that. We lived in a shitty, run-down trailer park back then, so the land was a pleasant surprise. I like to think he had intended to give me the land as a birthday gift that day we were supposed to go fishing, before everything went wrong. It makes me feel better. At least I got to tell him about Mary.

My writing career started taking off not long after Dad died. I stopped caring what people thought and started writing for myself. I dialed up the blood, gore, sex, and other depraved things. I poured all my emotions, anger, and grief into my stories, and it paid off. Sure, bloody and disgusting is entertaining, but you need a story in there, too. Emotions. Well-rounded character arcs. Shit like that. My books sold.

I wished Dad could see my success.

I had a good life, and I wouldn't change a thing about certain things. Me and Mary had a son, Hunter, who has grown up way too fast, as kids always seem to do. And I guess it was inevitable, but around book twenty-four, maybe-twenty-five, I fell into some trouble with writer's block—that, I would change in a heartbeat. Where once the ideas poured out, I started having problems coming up with stories, and when I did, I couldn't make the words flow like I used to. I limped along like this for a while, recycling my old plots—at first my readers didn't seem to give a fuck and kept buying. But when sales dipped on book thirty with no improvements in my mojo, I got nervous.

I had to face facts: I was an author who made a living writing extreme horror novels and I couldn't fucking write anything.

CHAPTER 2

MARY AND I BUILT a house on the land Dad left me, and not long after, two fans named Jackson and Jody showed up and stayed for a whole day. They wanted to hang out, get my autograph and chit-chat. Jackson was a short dude with long blond dreadlocks. He couldn't have been much over five foot five. Reminded me of a surfer dude. Jody was shorter, the same hair color. No dreadlocks though. Lots of piercings and tattoos. They kinda freaked me out at first but weren't being creepy or pushy or anything so I decided to let them stay for the day. It was my first exposure to obsessed fans, so I kinda liked it. I cleared it with Mary first, of course. I don't have a death wish. She'd kill me if I just up and let some strangers hang out at our house. We talked about my work, and I signed some copies of my books that they had brought with them. I invited them to come back any time. Even Mary liked them, which is unusual. She is not a people person. She was also pregnant at the time with our second child. Maybe the fluctuating hormones influenced how she felt.

I don't know why, but I've always wanted to live underground. This desire fed my obsession with doomsday bunkers. Maybe all those times I read *The Hobbit* had something to do with it, or all the zombie movies I've seen. I don't know. Maybe, I'm fucking weird. The next month, Jackson and Jody came to visit again and I mentioned my obsession. I had no idea they would actually build something for me. Joke was on me though. Jackson was a contractor, and had his own backhoe and construction equipment. He said if I paid for the materials, they would build it. So I did, and they started building. I tried to help at first, but I don't know jack about shit, so I just checked on the progress now and again. We lost the baby about halfway through construction and it fucked Mary up. She was often miserable and sad, and lost interest in sex, while my sex drive went the opposite direction. I didn't push the issue. Instead I started jerking off in the bathroom, and fantasizing about Jody.

Jody liked to wear black clothes, especially miniskirts and stockings. My Achilles heel. From the moment I first saw her, I wanted to bend her over and fuck her. Her and Jackson worked on the bunker for a couple years. They would have been done sooner but they had other shit to do too, and only came out here on weekends. It was good for me though. I probably dumped a thousand loads down the toilet thinking of her. One day I forgot to lock the bathroom and Mary caught me jerking off. She yelled at me. Her excuse was she didn't want Hunter to walk in and see that. I tried to tell her that I usually lock the door but she was so adamant I stopped whacking it in the house.

I went outside. Jackson was working on a little shed over the bunker hatch, heard the yelling, and wanted to know what happened. I don't know why but I told him the whole story. Thought he'd be pissed. I was wrong. Turns out they were a polyamorous couple and both bisexual. He said he'd suck my dick in the shed if I needed some release. I was tempted, but declined. As an added bonus, turns out I'm Jody's hall pass and once the bunker started to take shape I actually got to fuck her. Quite a few times. Sometimes, Jackson would watch and play with his little ding dong. I gave in after a few months of him asking and let him suck me off. It wasn't too bad, but I'd rather have pussy any day. One of these days, I hope to talk my wife into swapping with them.

Fuck.

I'm getting hard thinking about it.

I'm not obsessed with the end of the world or zombies or anything dumb like that. I genuinely like being underground. It makes me feel safe. With all the shit going on in the world, I could go down to the bunker and chill out and not worry about a fucking thing. I would stay down there all the time if I could.

Once complete, the bunker became my favorite place. It was perfect for writing, although by then I hadn't written a word in months. Sometimes, I went down there for the privacy and to beat off. Mary knew I did it, and didn't mind. I got tired of doing it in the shower or early in the morning when everyone slept. Sometimes, I got in the mood during the day, and that was when the bunker came in handy. I'd been married so long that fucking my wife had become a chore and was never spontaneous. After the miscarriage she changed a lot, and her pussy was a no-go most of the time. Usually, she was not in the mood or had some excuse not to do it unless it was late at night when Hunter was asleep and I was too tired. Maybe she planned it that way.

My sex drive is still high, even though I'm forty-five, and my imagination knows no bounds. I used to try to get Mary to let me bring another guy home so I could watch him fuck her, but she refused. I brought up the subject of swapping with Jackson and Jody and she told me I just wanted to fuck Jody. Other times, I wanted to role-play, but my ideas were always too extreme, like wanting her to play dead while I played horny morgue tech. Or have her play a prostitute,

and I pick her up and bang her behind a dumpster somewhere. I should have started with something simpler and
worked my way up, or told her it was research for a story.
But in the end it's easier to watch porn and take care of
myself than to get her to go along.

Mary hated the bunker at first, but warmed to it once she
saw progress and how nice it turned out. It's outfitted with
a ladder going down to the supply area, and that leads to the
kitchen/living room, then the bathroom. A tube design.
The bedroom is at the end with an adjoining office, or at
least that's what I call it. Really the office is just a nook with
a bookshelf in the corner and a glass drafting table I picked
up at a thrift store years ago that I use as a desk. I wrote my
best work on it, and this glass table and me will never part.

CHAPTER 3

HUNTER STARTED HIGH SCHOOL, freeing up my days. I make a point of going down to the bunker around nine and leaving at five, like regular work hours. I tell Mary I am writing. Most of the time, I'm watching porn. The weirder, the better. Since writing is how I make a living, she is okay with me spending time down there and even brings my mail down and leaves it in the kitchenette. I've tried talking her into letting me stick my dick in her. *You know*, I reason, *since you're already here*. But so far, *No*. I should start another project with Jackson and Jody. Then I wouldn't have to bother Mary about sex. I know she doesn't want to fuck as much as I do, and I feel bad asking. I do sneak Jackson and Jody down here sometimes for some fun when Mary isn't home. Her friend Donna lives a few miles away, and sometimes they get together to drink and have bonfires and shit. I keep hoping she'll come home with her pussy full of cum from the friend's husband, but so far that hasn't happened.

Aside from wanting to cum all the time, another odd thing I do is keep a framed letter from a stalker on my desk along with his picture. I keep it there to remind me of a bad time in my life, and how I need to be careful with fans.

Dakota Blackwell, I'll never forget him. Short black hair, tall, with muscles that made me a little jealous. This idiot had *my* face tattooed on his left butt cheek. He was certifiable. In and out of trouble. Went to jail once for beating up a girlfriend. Lived in his parents' basement. No job. Had nothing better to do than read my books and obsess over me. I would see him everywhere I went. At the gas station, the grocery store, the doctor's office. He found my house and came here every day. He would knock on the door nonstop. I filed so many police reports I could publish a whole book of them.

I finally had to get a restraining order, but it didn't work. Dakota was persistent, obsessed. He kept breaking the restraining order. Day after day, he harassed us. I bought a gun. Pulled it on him once. My hands were shaking so bad. I didn't want to have to take a life, but I would if I had to. The cops would come and he would already be gone sometimes—other times they'd drag him off in handcuffs.

He always came back.

I decided the only way he was going to leave us alone was if I killed him. I planned it, and was ready. I was tired of him. I feel like somehow he knew, because he stopped showing up. I got worried and couldn't sleep. I stayed up on the couch, gun in lap, in case he appeared. I thought about moving the family into the bunker, but how would we escape if he got in?

The last time he came, he brought his own gun. He was waving it around and shooting it in the air. He kept saying that he loved me and was my soul mate. We were all scared to death. I had my hand on the door handle and my weapon in the other. I was going to kill this son of a whore, but Mary stopped me. Said she needed me. Didn't want me to go to jail, or get killed.

I called the police. They tried to talk him down but he went nuts and shot at them. One of the cops took a bullet in the gut. He bled out before the ambulance could get here. When they finally subdued Dakota, they beat him within an inch of his life.

After he was sentenced to life for the murder of a police officer, I finally got some relief and stability back. He was fucked now. The cops said he'd never get out of jail. I used to call the prison to find out if he was still alive, and eventually during one of those calls they told me he had passed away. I don't know if he was butt-raped to death, but I certainly hope so. He deserved it for what he did to us. That bastard nearly ruined our lives, and killed a cop on my front lawn. The whole ordeal gave me ulcers and panic attacks. Mary's hair started falling out from the stress. We all went to therapy for a long time after that. I like to think he is rotting in hell, skin melting off his flesh as the eternal fire slowly eats away at his body. I wanted to go down into the bunker for the rest of my life, but Mary wouldn't have it. As usual, she was right. After a while my fear subsided and we returned to some semblance of a good life. They say time heals all wounds, but I still think about it when I look at the letter—and that bastard's picture.

People send a lot of shit for me to sign, books they've bought and other merchandise. Sometimes, it's shirts, pictures, and on the occasion, used panties and bras. Sometimes dildos. I will sign anything. I keep the lingerie. I've shot a bunch of loads in fans' used panties over the years. I never wash them either. I don't want to spoil the flavor. Some of the garments still smell like pussy. I keep them in a lockbox in my big desk drawer, and I'll use them until they fall apart. I hope the wife never finds them. Cum stains on a fan's used lingerie might be a deal breaker for her. She already hates it when I jizz on her stuff.

As far as my career, I have been looking for a comeback, a new book, or even a novella. I have been "writing" in the bunker for nearly a month with nothing to show. I better come up with something fast before Mary gets suspicious.

Every day, I sit at my desk with my hands on my keyboard and nothing comes out. I have a title, but that's it. *Absorbed By Excrement*. It's a great title, but that's all I have.

It's frustrating to be a writer and unable to write. I've considered hiring a ghostwriter, but the thought is appalling. Hopefully, I will never get that desperate. I don't know why the words won't flow. They used to come so quick. Maybe I'm burned out. I have no idea. I could resort to the convention circuit if worse came to worse and I get desperate for money, but I'm too antisocial to make a real go at conventions. Maybe I could do OnlyFans.

That pretty much brings us up to the present.

CHAPTER 4

I PICKED UP A small package on the desk to my right in the pile of mail that Mary had left for me. The return address read *From A Fan*. I ripped it open and reached inside. To my surprise, it was a picture of me from years ago taken by the stalker. I remember it clearly because it had been published in the newspaper. Creepy. I wondered, *Why the fuck would someone send me this?* It wasn't a dirty picture, just me mowing the yard, shirtless. It's the fact that fucker took it of me while hiding in the woods near my house that gets to me.

I shoved the picture in the trash can under my desk along with the packaging. Some of the garbage spilled onto the floor. I bent down to pick it up. That was the exact moment my phone yelled at me. I shit myself a little and hit my head on the desk as I came up.

"God Dammit!" I yelled, prying the phone out of my pocket with one hand and rubbing my head with the other.

My wife had installed a screaming goat ringtone on my phone as a joke, and I didn't know how to change it. Once, it went off in Walmart and scared an old lady so bad she tipped and fell over and I had to catch her. I couldn't help but laugh. She thought I was an asshole for laughing. *Jeez, lady, I could have let you hit the floor,* I remember thinking. But I didn't say it. I'm a nice guy.

I opened the phone to check the message: *Lunch is ready.* I replied: *Be there in a minute.*

This was new. Usually, Mary brings a sandwich down to me. My insides gurgled. I didn't realize I was hungry. Time flies when you're accomplishing nothing. I got up from the desk, stretched my arms and legs, walked down the hallway to the ladder, and climbed up.

In the kitchen, I sat down to a surprise. Mary had made chicken fettuccine alfredo, my favorite. It was delicious. Homemade sauce, too, not that cheap crap from a jar. This was some serious shit. She smiled from across the table, and I noticed she had brushed her hair and put on makeup. She rarely does that anymore, so I assumed something was up. Either she wanted something, or I was about to be pissed off. She was wearing a robe, and her hair was a little damp. She must have recently showered. I ate fast. My dad used to say, *if you eat quick, you'll get dessert sooner,* and I've eaten that way ever since.

"This is great, honey, thanks," I said between mouthfuls.

"You're welcome."

"I really appreciate it. It's delicious."

She smiled. We sat silently. I wolfed down my food, and she barely touched hers. She never ate a lot, but still, her behavior was suspicious, like she was going to ask me to buy her something expensive. I finished cleaning my plate with a piece of garlic bread, and she looked at me sheepishly. "I thought maybe we could fool around, since Hunter is at the lake."

I shoved the last piece of garlic bread in my mouth. "Really?" I asked, chewing.

"Yeah, but brush your teeth. I don't want your garlic breath in my face."

"You got it," I said.

I didn't expect that. It had been a long time since Mary initiated sex. It was usually me. I got up and ran to the bathroom to brush my teeth. I noticed her at the door. Her robe fell. She was naked. My dick sprang to attention. She raised an eyebrow.

I rinsed my mouth and followed her luscious, swaying cheeks into the bedroom, stripping my clothes off as I went. Mary ran the rest of the way, and by the time I got there, I was nude except for my socks. I hate being barefoot. Sounds weird, but I keep them on during sex. She was bent over with her elbows on the bed, and her back arched down.

She looked back at me. "You like it like this, don't you?" I didn't bother to answer. My mind was on one thing. I was so horny I grabbed her hips and slid right in. She was wet, but it didn't feel natural. She must have lubed herself beforehand. I didn't care. I was in heaven. I almost came. I held still, savoring the feeling of being inside her. It didn't happen as often as I would like. I couldn't wait any longer and began sliding in and out. Her muscles clamped down on my cock, and I came. I nearly fainted.

"No fair!" I said.

She laughed as I pulled out. I watched the cum drip out of her pussy, licking my lips as she lay down and rolled over onto her back. I imagined it was another guy's cum, and I got hard again. I climbed on top of her.

The second time, I lasted longer.

CHAPTER 5

A N HOUR LATER, I was descending the ladder to the bunker feeling energized. I'd finally gotten laid. Twice. Mary was a little annoyed that I got hard again so soon after the first time, but it had been a while, and I took advantage of the situation. I was right though. She wanted something. A new car. She was tired of her old one, she said. It had a hundred and fifty thousand miles and was starting to fall apart. Of course, she didn't bring it up until after sex. She knows how to get what she wants, and I do love her, so I don't mind buying her stuff.

After I fucked her and promised we would go pick her out a new car, she fell asleep. I felt good, so I showered and went back down to the bunker. Maybe good sex was the spark I needed to get a story going.

When I sat back down at the desk, I was shocked and irritated to see that someone had written a few paragraphs under my title. *What the fuck? Who came down here? Did I write something and forget about it?* I doubt I would forget that. Someone must be fucking with me, but who? Hunter, maybe. I bet he was home and pranking me. He does that sometimes. I don't usually mind, but my one rule has always been to stay away from my desk and don't fuck with my computer. I sighed. Guess I'll have to have a talk with him later.

Out of curiosity, I read what he had written:

Absorbed By Excrement
Part 1

JUSTIN KICKED OPEN THE bathroom door behind the Phillips 66 gas station where he worked. Rushing in, he stood before the toilet and fumbled with the buttons on his pants. The cheesy beef enchiladas he'd eaten a half hour earlier were screaming at his butthole. An anal explosion was imminent, and if he didn't get the pants out of the way they would soon be filled with creamy, warm diarrhea. He should have known. The food here always gave him the shits. Thank Christ, the bathroom wasn't occupied.

"Oh, God," he whispered as he finally figured out his buttons. He dropped his pants and turned to sit on the toilet. As a volcano of wet shit exploded from his anus, he felt something cold and slimy where his ass cheeks and legs met the toilet seat. Disgusted, he shot to his feet and slipped while continuing to spray diarrhea. Turning back, he saw someone had vomited all over the toilet seat and bathroom floor. He almost puked. It would have been comical had his head not hit the toilet with a dull thud. He lay out cold in the foul combination of excrement and vomit as the steady spray shooting out of his ass slowed.

Minutes later, he awoke with a splitting headache to the sound of someone pounding on the door. He lifted his head with a groan and when the miasma of revolting smells wafted up to fuck his nostrils, he added his own vomit to the collection on the floor. When he realized what he was lying in, he stood, desperate to hold it in at both ends. His pants, still around his ankles, were soaked in the vile-smelling combination of liquids.

He wobbled and almost fell again, but managed to grab onto the sink to support himself. It felt like someone was hammering a nail in his forehead, and he reached up to touch the sore spot.

His hand came away covered in blood, shit, and bits of enchilada.

I leaned back in my chair and thought about it. The writing was kind of dumb, and I'm not sure Hunter would come up with something like this. On the other hand, it was the type of weird shit I looked for in a story—and more important, this was the gross stuff that sold my books. I wished the story was mine.

But who's to say it wasn't? The writing turned up on my computer, after all. Maybe I had hammered it out in one of those fugue states people talk about and just forgot I'd done so. I thought about the possibilities of where I could go with it, and my mind opened, flooding with ideas. Fuck yeah.

The laptop made a loud beeping sound. Words appeared on the screen under the three paragraphs:

What do you think? Good, huh?

They disappeared.

Alarmed, I rose and backed away from the desk. That was fucked up. Either I was going crazy, or someone had hacked my laptop. The only person who could do that would be Hunter. The little shit. *He must be fucking with me.* That's all I could think. *He and his friends are probably in his room laughing at me.*

"Is this a prank? You're watching through the webcam and fucking with me, right? Hunter, is that you?" I asked, approaching the computer.

No more words came. I pushed the power button. Nothing happened. I tried again and held it down, but still nothing. I couldn't turn it off. My patience wore thin. I didn't take kindly to people playing jokes on me, and this was already getting old. Hunter would know that.

I opened the top drawer of my desk, retrieved a dark blue sticky note, and plastered it over the camera. At least they couldn't see me now. "All right Hunter, knock it off or..." I began, before more words appeared on the screen.

I'm not Hunter, and it powers off when I say it powers off.

"Who the fuck are you then?" I pounded my fist on the desk.

I stared, livid, as the words kept coming..

Calm down, Joshua. I'm just a fan. In fact, I'm your biggest fan. I have read every word you have published and more. Like I said, I want a story by you for my collection. One that's only for me, no one else.

"Why don't you write your own story?"

I'm not a writer. You are. I know everything about you, and you have forgotten about me, I'm sure. I went to jail for you. You said I was stalking you, but I know better. We were meant to be together, you and me. I'm going to prove it to you.

Besides, you owe me. Now, take this story intro and finish it. Or I will do something drastic.

"Nice try, whoever you are. Dakota Blackwell is long dead," I said.

Yes, I died, and I have returned. I'm different now. Much different. Give me what I want, and I will leave you alone.

I broke out in a cold sweat and ground my teeth. Perspiration chilled my body while the phantom words sank in.

I swallowed, hoping it was a joke. It had to be.

"What if I just leave and burn this place to the ground?" I asked.

I wouldn't allow that. I am tired of arguing. Get to work. Now.

"How do I know you're telling the truth?"

I guess I will have to prove myself. Tiresome, but so be it. Come closer.

I leaned forward, my nose almost touching the screen.

"Is something supposed to be happening?" I laughed.

A red hand shot through the screen and grabbed me by the throat. It was covered in burnt skin, blood, and scabs. Sharp, talon-like nails cut into my skin, leaving blood trails trickling down my neck. The hand squeezed, cutting off my breath. I tried to break free, but it was too strong. I pulled on the arm. It didn't budge. I balled my hands into fists and hit the arm repeatedly as hard as I could. The skin was leather-hard. The grip tightened on my throat.

Just as I thought I might pass out for lack of oxygen, the hand released me and disappeared inside the screen. I gasped for breath, loudly sucking in air. Fuck my life.

Do you believe me now?

I panted, recovering from the shock of near-strangulation. "Yes, I believe you. Jesus, you almost choked me to death!"

Think about this: If I can do that, I can do other things too. Worse things.

I touched the side of my neck. My fingers came away with blood.

"Okay, okay. You win. You have my attention."

I was so scared I almost shit myself, and my butthole got *real* itchy. The hand could have crushed my neck like a lion chomping down on a wildebeest's throat.

"Why are you doing this?"

I will get the joy of seeing your work come to life, and it's the only way I feel I can cross over to the other side. I am stuck here, on this plane of existence. Neither dead nor alive, and I wish to be free. My master won't let me leave here until my mission is complete. Perhaps he will release me if I do well. It is my hope.

"What if I don't want to dance to your tune?"

Like I said, I know everything about you, even when you're down in the bunker, or up in your house. I know where you are and what you are doing. I also know your son is on his way home. He was fishing at the lake with his friends. I can see them walking down a forest path. I know that your wife is asleep upstairs in your bedroom with two loads of your cum soaking her white cotton panties. They could both be dead before you made it up the ladder. Their deaths would come with the ease of suffocating a baby with a pillow.

Do you want that?

Do you need proof that I can kill as well?

"No, I don't."

Then sit down and write.

I considered the situation. There was little else I could do, no way could I say no to a supernatural being that could kill us whenever it wanted. I had no choice but to write the story. I sighed. At least I was writing again.

"If I write this, will you leave us alone?"

You will never hear from me again. If that is your wish.

"Okay, I'll do it."

Make it good.

I rolled my eyes and reread the two paragraphs he had written to get a feel for the story and an idea of what direction to take. I typed:

29

Absorbed By Excrement
Part 2

Whoever was outside pounded on the door. "Come on, man! I gotta shit!"

"Hold on, I'll be out in a minute!" Justin hollered back.

He kicked his pants off, slipped the shirt over his head, and used it to scrape as much of the unholy liquids off himself as possible. He took off his shoes and socks and tossed them under the sink, followed by the rest of his clothes. He rinsed his head and face in the too-small ceramic bowl before attempting to clean his clothes in the sink. More pounding. This time, the hinges moved as the door shook. *Doesn't this idiot realize it's occupied?*

"I'm in here! Are you fucking deaf?" Justin said.

"Bro, I'm about to shit myself, and you've been in there at least fifteen minutes!"

"Fuck off somewhere else, man. You don't wanna come in here anyway!"

"There is nowhere else!"

"Shit outside asshole!"

Justin finished rinsing the wound on his head and made a feeble attempt at unclogging the sink before continuing to wash himself. He was getting used to the smell and leaned over the sink to rinse his arms off as the man outside violently kicked the door. It looked like it would burst open at any second.

"Let me in there before I kick this door down!"

"I'm in here, you piece of shit! Fuck off!"

He bent over to pick up his shoes and socks as the door burst open. A giant man wearing a long-sleeved plaid shirt and overalls stood slack-jawed in the doorway. He was at least six feet tall and well over four hundred pounds. The flab at his sides spilled out of his overalls. On his head was a red hat cocked over to one side. When the man saw the condition of the bathroom and the naked asshole winking at him, his eyes grew wide.

Consumed with the shame of being seen in such a compromising position, Justin couldn't help it and let loose with another volley of anal artillery, blasting his ass vomit all over the man. Most of it hit the dude's overalls and dripped down to his boots, but a little got in his beard.

Roaring in anger, the man leaned forward, retched, and put a hand up to his mouth to try to stop it, but the vomit spewed out all over his face and beard. "Fuck!" he exclaimed, the vomit sliding down his chin.

"I told you not to come in here!" Justin squeaked.

"Goddammit! If it didn't smell so bad in there, I'd kick your ass! What the fuck is wrong with you? Jesus Christ!" The man turned to leave, looked back, and yelled, "I'm calling the cops man!"

The big man lumbered off and stopped a few feet away to blow chunks on the ground before moving on.

"Wait! Please!" Justin pleaded.

The man was already out of earshot.

Justin closed the door, looked down at the mess he had created, and sighed, wondering how one man could hold such a volume of shit in his bowels. What would the police think if they saw this?

He decided he had better throw on his nasty clothes and get the fuck out before they showed up.

Starting with the shirt, he gagged as it slid across his head. When he pulled up his pants, he felt an unfamiliar sensation on his buttocks. Something crawled over his ass. Reaching around, he shoved a hand in his pants to feel around for it. He brushed against what felt like a slimy, worm-like creature as it disappeared into his crack, heading for his anus. He frantically dug deeper to get it, but whatever it was, it moved too fast and had slithered inside his body, followed by the tip of his finger, which he withdrew. It was too late. Justin felt the creature squirming around inside him.

He let his pants drop and looked down in bewilderment as his dick hardened. Whatever it was, hit his sweet spot. It slowly worked past the prostate and through his bowels, the large and small intestine, and finally stopped in his stomach. He reached around to finger his asshole again, and with his other hand, grabbed his cock. He furiously masturbated, not caring that he was smearing shit all up and down his member.

"Oh fuck, it's never felt so good," he whispered.

As he neared climax, someone politely knocked on the door. In his surprise he stopped jerking off but his dick remained hard. He wanted to cum so bad it hurt, and his stomach felt full as the pressure built.

"Anyone in there?" the voice on the other side of the door asked.

Justin didn't care and didn't bother to answer. Whatever was happening to him had made him so horny all he wanted to do was cum. He started to jerk his cock again. The pressure increased so much that his insides hurt, but still, he kept going. His guts twisted with pain as he neared climax.

"Are you okay? It's Sheriff Borland," the voice said from outside.

Justin had a fleeting thought—*He got here fast*—before returning to the business at hand.

An overwhelming urge to blow ass again overcame him and he no longer gave a flying fuck who was at the door. He groaned in pain, thinking he would vomit again, and turned toward the toilet, still violently masturbating. But nothing came up when he retched. It was getting harder to breathe, and the pain in his guts got worse fast. Hunching down over the toilet, he put his free hand on his abdomen. It had distended so much that it looked like he was nine months pregnant. He felt like he would split open. Euphoric pain swelled inside him.

"No, I'm fine!" he screamed.

The creature growing within him pushed against his anus and expanded. He felt his bunghole tearing and screamed in agony as it crowned, stretching the orifice at an incredible speed.

Looking down at his midsection, he saw a line forming where the skin was stretching and ripping apart. Little holes of flesh opened up like Swiss cheese, and his abdomen split in two halves as he came.

"All right. I'm coming in."

The sheriff busted down the door and was greeted by a head hanging out of a man's ass. Blood shot out of the shit-covered cock while the body slid apart. The shocked sheriff watched, unable to rip his eyes away, as the two halves of what remained of the ravaged man's body glided to the floor. The cock was pointed up, shooting spurts of blood like a macabre fountain. In the middle of the split, bloodied body stood a small semi-humanoid figure made entirely from feces and vomit. Before the sheriff's eyes, the creature expanded. Had the sheriff's brain the time to process what his eyes were taking in, he may have formed the thought, *Jesus, this guy just birthed a shit monster.* But there was no such time.

The creature sniffed around, and, noticing Justin's body, reached out with an arm-like appendage and touched half of the split corpse. It sucked the flesh into its body and grew larger, then repeated the process with the other half. The corpse's penis and the bloody meat surrounding it were the last to disappear inside the creature's body, going in with a spectacular slurping noise.

When it finished consuming its host, the shit monster stood as tall as a man.

"Christ!" the sheriff said.

The monster's head snapped toward the sound of the sheriff's voice, and it slowly raised itself to its full height. The overpowering smell worsened. The sheriff covered his mouth and nose with his left hand and backed away as the shit monster slid toward him, gliding across the slime like a giant, upright slug.

With his right hand, the sheriff reached for his weapon and unclasped it. He clicked off the safety and pointed it at the creature.

CHAPTER 6

I PAUSED TO STRETCH my arms above my head and crack my knuckles. I was getting into the story now. Parts of it made my dick hard. The sign of a good work is that it evokes feelings. Even if the feelings are in my cock. I stood, paced, and checked my phone. Mary had sent me a link to a developing news story. I was about to tap it when the laptop beeped, and I focused on the screen.

More words:

Finish the story. You can look at that bullshit later. Or I will make you watch as I slit your wife's throat.

The words disappeared.

"Okay, just hold on. I'll finish it. I just needed a little break."

I sat down, took a deep breath, and began again:

Absorbed By Excrement
Part 3

The sheriff pulled his chrome and pearl handled revolver from his side holster and fired two shots at the thing's abdomen, but the bullets disappeared into the monster's bulk. The shots only pissed it off. It roared and lunged for him. Retreating, the sheriff darted through the door and into the open, reaching for his shoulder mic to call for backup. The beast advanced toward him. The creature mesmerized him—the combination of shit, jizz, and blood swirling around, cycling throughout its body like a hypnotist's spiral.

The sheriff clicked on the mic. "I need help at the gas station, fast. In the back where the men's room is," he whispered.

"Sheriff?" The voice that answered sounded concerned.

"Send help, now!"

"Copy that."

The radio crackled.

He stepped away as the shit monster slithered forward, leaving a sizable brown streak in its wake. Having witnessed how quickly this thing had absorbed Justin, the sheriff moved faster. *If it touches me I'll be shit monster fodder,* he thought, not registering that he had, at last, given the creature a name. It would be his last clear thought. His foot connected with the curb and he fell into some bushes. The monster picked up speed and was upon him.

The sheriff froze.

"Help!"

No one was around to hear.

He didn't know what to do. He hadn't been trained to deal with this. No one had. He could manage theft, murder, and dumbass people forgetting how to drive, but this was a whole new level. His heart pounded. He felt pressure in his chest as he tried to get up, but the creature was already there, standing over him.

"Oh, God, not like this!"

It reached down, grabbed him by the neck, and lifted him. The smell was putrescent, like a mixture of wet dog, diarrhea, and a dead skunk that had rotted on the road for three weeks, baking in the sun. He fought the urge to blow chunks. With his oxygen cut off, he flailed around and kicked, trying to get loose, but its grip held firm. In a final, dim realization, the sheriff understood he was about to die at the hands of a shit monster and there was nothing he could do about it. His body trembled as the thing pulled him forward into itself in a grisly kind of embrace, then Sheriff Borland began sinking into the creature. Inch by inch, he disappeared into the shit monster, feeling his body parts burning, miraculously still living, still registering excruciating pain as they plunged slowly into the abomination. Soon, only the sheriff's head remained outside. He let out a final bloodcurdling scream as his body was fully absorbed.

The shit monster made a satisfied huffing sound as it slowly withdrew toward the bathroom. Halfway there, it stopped, raised its head toward the sky, and made a loud, gurgling howl before proceeding back through the bathroom door, where it waited.

It wouldn't have to wait long.

A siren wailed in the distance.

More victims were on the way.

I stopped typing, the story was finished.

Finally, I had written something. It was under duress, but I was proud of it. Back in business, I smiled, rose, and paced in front of the desk, waiting for my tormentor to say something. The wait turned into minutes. I ground my teeth back and forth. It felt like someone running nails down a chalkboard. This shit was driving me insane.

The screen beeped.

I sat.

That part where he gave birth to the butt baby and it ripped him in half was brilliant. Well done. The blood-spurting cock fountain. Genius.

"Umm...thanks? Does this mean you'll fuck off back to wherever you came from?" I asked.

Like Shakespeare said, my word is my bond.

The story disappeared off the screen.

It was over.

Dakota was gone, or his spirit was gone, or whatever the fuck it was. Better than that, I got my mojo back. It felt good to write again. Hopefully, I was out of my slump and could get back to work.

CHAPTER 7

I DECIDED TO CHECK on Mary. Hunter would be back any minute also. I headed down the hall and hustled up the ladder and opened the hatch. Climbing out, I scanned the yard. The thought struck me that someone who didn't know the bunker was there would probably freak out seeing a man's head emerge. That made me laugh, an insane sounding cackle that barely sounded like me, and that's when I saw Hunter with a couple of his friends from school, putting his fishing gear in the shed on the other side of the yard. He looked up and waved. If he noticed anything off about me, he didn't show it.

"Hey, bud," I said, waving back.

"We're going to the movies after this. Is that okay?"

"That's fine. Just be careful."

"I know," he said.

He went back to what he was doing. He and his buddies laughed as I walked toward the house. These days, Hunter had little time for me. He recently got his driver's license and a car. I let him pick it out. It was an old blue Honda Civic. I heard those things last forever, and are tough. A perfect first car, and if he wrecks it, that's okay. It's not like it's a Tesla or something fancy. It had cost more than I wanted to pay, but at least I didn't have to drive him around anymore. I walked to the house and entered through the sliding glass door to the living room, where Mary sat, watching the news on the couch. She patted the sofa, and I joined her.

"Honey, listen to this. Something is going on at Phillips 66," she said.

I slid closer to her and put my arm around her shoulder. Something *was* happening at the gas station, and it looked all too familiar. A news helicopter gave a bird's-eye shot of the shit monster I had just brought to life in my story. Staring at the screen in disbelief, I removed my arm from Mary's shoulder and sat forward. The creature appeared exactly as I had imagined it, down to the last detail.

"I gotta warn Hunter not to leave."

I pushed to my feet and sprinted to the front door, flinging it open in time to see Hunter driving off. Frantically, I dug into my pocket for my phone. It wasn't there. I must have left it in the bunker.

"Mary, call Hunter. He's headed right toward that thing!" I shouted.

Grabbing her phone from between her legs, she dialed, and then held it to her ear. Watching Mary, I chewed my fingernails. She bit her lower lip.

Precious seconds passed.

"Well?" I asked.

She shook her head. "He isn't answering." She turned toward the TV. "Oh God, look!"

I stared, gaping at the unfolding scene. Several people in hazmat suits stood by while a dozen police officers shot at the shit monster. The bullets had no effect and were absorbed into its body, and I swear, it grew a little with each round. In the background, I saw Hunter's Honda pull into the parking lot. *What the fuck is he doing?*

I looked up in time to see a pair of legs sink into the creature's side, and it continued to expand. It was at least twelve feet tall now, and still growing. A brown tendril reached out from its body, picked up the nearest police officer, and raised him to its face. The mouth opened, stretching wider than the man's body and exposing several rows of long, sharp teeth made from, Jesus were those human ribs? Now, it was evolving beyond what I'd written. Hunter was out of his car and stood in the background with his friends. What the fuck. They were pointing their phones at it. The shit monster dropped the officer into its mouth and chomped him in half.

Mary turned toward me.

"You saw all that, right?" I said.

"Should we drive there and get Hunter?"

I turned the volume down so I could think. *I should probably go down there. That might get me killed too, but it would be worth it to save Hunter. But if what I had written came to life, Dakota Blackwell is somehow responsible. I'm sure of it. That means he could reverse it!*

I hoped.

I jumped as the television gave off a deep, guttural roar. The reporter was hightailing it away from the gas station, still trying to do her story. The picture shook as the camera operator ran down the dirt road toward our house. The sound kept cutting out. I could barely make out the creature in the background. It had grown larger.

Fuck.

"Jessica Rutledge for Channel Six News. Do not come anywhere near Lake Eucha or the surrounding area! The Phillips 66 on the highway...giant monster...feces everywhere...dead police officers...absorbed by... You heard me right. Avoid the area! A giant monster made of dookie is sucking up everyone in its path. Before we were forced to flee, we had received word that the Army is on its way and..."

The channel cut out.

"Josh, we need to do something!" Mary cried.

"Stay here in case Hunter calls. I have an idea," I said.

"Where are you going?"

A loud vibration shook the house. I ignored her and ran outside. Looking up, I heard the heavy thrumming of helicopters. They came into view, flying low over the trees approaching the gas station. It was the military. I hoped that Hunter had come to his senses and got out of there before the shit went down.

Dakota Blackwell wasn't done with me.

"What's happening?" Mary shrieked from the doorway.

"It's the Army. Go back inside. They'll handle everything." I pushed her back into the house and shut the door.

Sprinting across the backyard, I threw open the bunker's hatch and climbed down the ladder. I rushed down the hall to the bedroom and sat at the desk. The computer glowed, and Microsoft Word stood open on the screen. But the document was completely blank.

"All right, you son of a bitch. What is happening? The military is about to fucking nuke everything!"

Do you like it?

"No, I don't like it! Army helicopters just buzzed my house! What did you do?"

Nothing much. You wrote the story. I brought it to life. I thought that would make you happy.

"Brought it to life?"

Yeah, pretty cool seeing your work in real life?

"No, not cool. People are dying. That thing will devour the whole planet if you don't stop it!"

I don't want to stop it. I want you to suffer like I have suffered.

"Don't you care that people will die? What about your parents?"

No, they were terrible people. I do care about you though. You're the only one I care about. Your books were my whole life. I love you. If the world gets destroyed, then we can be together. Forever.

"If you love me, fix it. I'll do anything. I don't want to die, and I don't want my family to die. I may have turned you in but you got killed in jail—it wasn't me."

I know. Maybe I am being too hard on you, but this all has a purpose. You will see.

"No, I won't see. My son is in danger. He drove there, and for all I know he's being eaten by that thing."

The stress headache this was causing would soon require more than the recommended dose of Tylenol. Here I was, arguing with my dead-not-dead stalker through a computer, and I realized I had yet to ask the most important question. "How the fuck are you making what I write become real?"

Finally, a decent question. When I died, I went to hell, and you wouldn't believe how much fire is down there. I would burn and burn during the day until nothing was left, and the next day, I was whole again, and it started all over. Every day for years until he noticed me.

"Who noticed you?"

My master noticed me, and said he liked my resilience and how I never once complained about the fire, pain, and suffering. He said he had plans for me. The fire cleansed me, and I was ready to be set loose on the world and help him with his plan. You should feel good. You were my first stop. I have work to do, my master's work, and you are going to help.

"So, you're a fucking demon?"

How else do you think I can do what I do? He gave me power, and I am here to do his work. Any way I can, and what better way to corrupt the masses than through the words of a successful author. Your words reach millions. You have corrupted more souls than the master. That's why we need you working, churning out books. Converting the masses, one soul at a time. He will become so powerful that not even God can stop him.

"What you're saying is you want me to write books like I always have?"

Yes. So many people learn from your work. It gives them ideas for crimes so vile that my master can't help but get drunk with power. It's a blessing in disguise for the master. This story is practice, so you can get your writing back in shape. I think it's working. Don't you?

"Yeah, it's working. Are you here right now?"

I can be both physical and ethereal. I can be here and elsewhere.

"So, you can be up there watching my family while you are inside the computer talking to me?"

Yes.

"What do I have to do to end this shit?"

Funny you should say "shit," since that is the subject of your story.

"Tell me what to do."

Keep writing the story. Kill the monster and make it good. Make it believable. Make it so nasty and disturbing that people will remember it long after you die. Do that, and everything will go back to how it was before. Hurry, before the monster reaches you.

"Are you ever going to be done with me?"

When you finish.

"You said that before."

You will have to trust me.

The bunker shook and gunfire burst outside. That sounded way too close to home. My phone rang. Mary was probably scared out of her wits. I didn't bother answering.

When I should be shitting my pants, I felt only exhilaration. I should be ashamed to write such filth. I had never realized it before, but I guess I am doing the Devil's work. I should have been mortified, but I wasn't. This was fun. Exciting. The very thing my life had been lacking. The bunker shook again. Some of my books fell off the shelf. I realized I had better start writing fast, before the shit monster got to me. Gleefully, I considered where the story left off, and got to work:

Absorbed By Excrement
Part 4

Another police vehicle pulled up and parked next to Sheriff Borland's squad car in the Phillips 66 parking lot. The gas station stood in an odd location, situated at the bottom of a hill near Lake Eucha next to a bridge that cut across the water. On one side of the road was a forested area filled with evergreens and dotted with massive oaks, and on the other was a run-down trailer park that had seen better days. There was a time when people came from all around to visit the lake, but visitors had ebbed since the trailer park rolled into the area. From the highway it looked like a trash dump.

A tall, well-muscled police officer stepped out of the truck into the hot sun and took his sunglasses off to better survey the scene. *Delaware County Sheriff's Department* was emblazoned on the side of his vehicle. His golden nametag gleamed in the sunlight, reading C. Clinton in dark lettering. He strolled around his truck to inspect the sheriff's still-running car, reached in through the half-open window to turn the ignition off, and looked for signs of a struggle. On the floorboard were several empty beer cans and a half-drunk pint of cheap vodka. Finding no other evidence, he turned to the gas station. Everything looked normal. The only thing he expected to discover was the sheriff passed out. It wouldn't be the first time.

The sheriff had been dealing with a lot lately. His wife had died after a long battle with leukemia. Following that, he had lost his way and didn't know how to raise his daughter by himself, so he left her alone often, and she had to deal with the grief of losing her mom without him, which took a toll on her. Sometimes, he would leave her with his family, but they never let her stay long. Without a support system or any way to cope with her own pain, she began sneaking out at night and getting into trouble. She started taking pills, which they constantly argued about. On her eighteenth birthday, she took his car out while drunk and ended up getting into an accident that killed another driver. The sheriff was the first officer on the scene. She went to prison. The sheriff turned to alcohol to deal with it and spiraled out of control.

As the new man on the force, Deputy Clinton had more than once taken it upon himself to sober the sheriff up enough to get him home or back to the station. He didn't mind the babysitting duty—he got paid regardless. While Clinton assessed the scene, an old beat-up car pulled up to a gas pump near his truck. The driver, a short woman with bright red hair, went into the gas station and quickly returned, shaking her head as she walked to her car. Clinton wondered why someone would dye their hair such a color.

"Hey, did you see Sheriff Borland in there?" he asked.

"Ain't no one in there. I couldn't pay for my gas."

"Why don't you just pay at the pump?"

"Ain't got no card. I only use cash on account of I don't trust the banks and shit. Oh hell. I better tell ya, the smell in there. It's terrible—'bout tossed my cookies. I wonder if a sewer main broke or something?"

"I don't know, but I will find out. I can smell it out here."

"Yeah, worse inside. Aight, I gotta go. Good luck, officer."

"Thanks."

The missing clerk concerned Clinton. He knew the guy from high school, Justin Jones. Not really a friend, but a face he recognized when passing in the hallway. He approached the front door, opened it, and peeked through.

"Hello?"

No answer. Odd. He walked around the side of the building but saw nothing out of the ordinary. Just the rack of propane bottles that no one ever bought next to the ice cooler. The white paint on the wall was fading and falling off in flecks. A noise caught his ear and he rested his right hand on the grip of his holstered weapon. A rustling, like something crawling around in the leaves out in the woods. A squirrel, maybe. He held his breath and wiped sweat off his brow with the back of his left hand as he walked past the propane and the ice. Justin was hopefully busy taking a shit. Or trying to fix the sewer. The smell could almost reach out and slap a vulture off fresh roadkill. He wrinkled his nose in disgust as he rounded the building and stopped at the sight before him. A two-foot-wide brown trail led from the bathroom door to a bush dripping with hot and chunky wet feces.

Pressing a hand to his mouth to stifle a gag, Deputy Clinton approached the bush, where the brown trail seemed to open up into a pool of what he now realized was diarrhea. That explained the smell, but where the fuck were

Justin and the sheriff? He spotted a pistol down in the diarrhea-blasted bush. Definitely the sheriff's piece. He would recognize Pearl anywhere. The sheriff loved to talk about how he won her gambling on a dart game at his favorite bar before he moved to these parts from Austin. Clinton unclasped the strap over his gun and clicked off the safety. He turned toward the bathroom door, noting more diarrhea oozing out from under it. Dark trouble was brewing in that bathroom, and he wasn't about to face it alone. He clicked on his shoulder radio. "Eleven-twenty-two on the scene."

"Eleven-twenty-two go," the dispatcher replied.

"I found Pearl, but no sign of the sheriff."

"Do you think he is ten fifty-one?"

"I don't think he's drunk. This may be a ten zero-zero. There is some weird shit going on here. I mean, there is literal shit oozing out from under the bathroom door. Something happened to the sheriff, I know it. He doesn't leave Pearl anywhere, even when he's drunk. That's the thing he cares about the most."

"What do you mean there's shit oozing out of the door?" She sounded irritated.

"Something must be happening with the sewer. It's coming from under the door. And there is a trail of it from the door over to where I found the gun. Stinks to high heaven, too. Smells like a dog ate some shit, puked, ate the puke, and shit it out again."

"You have got to be kidding."

"I'll text you some pics."

"I'll check your body cam."

"That hasn't worked in months, and Delaware County's too cheap to buy new ones."

"Shit."

"I keep asking, and they keep denying."

"All right. Send me something. This, I gotta see to believe."

"Hope you haven't had lunch, because you might blow chunks."

"I can handle it."

"Suit yourself."

He pulled his phone from his pants pocket, snapped pics, and sent them to her. He recorded a quick video of the shit as it flowed out of the door and the trail to the sheriff's gun. He sent that too.

The radio crackled. "Jesus Christ, Clinton. That is disgusting!"

"Imagine smelling it," he said.

"No, thank you."

"Seriously, send help fast. I have no idea what the fuck is going on here."

"I'll send backup."

He backed away from the door and returned to his truck to wait. Producing a white handkerchief from his shirt pocket, he blotted his forehead. It was the beginning of summer in Oklahoma and hotter than a homeless woman's cooch on food stamp day. Wet, muggy, and miserable.

He climbed into the cab of his truck, turned up the AC, pulled a pack of Marlboros out of his shirt pocket, and lit one. Distant sirens rapidly approached as he took a long drag and exhaled. He sighed in relief, the nicotine calming his nerves. He took another drag as two police vehicles arrived and pulled up by his truck. He got out, took one last drag, flicked the cigarette down, and stomped it out. Too bad there wasn't time to smoke the whole thing. The officers got out of their vehicles.

"What's up, Clinton?" the first officer, Jeffries, asked while Eubanks approached from the other squad car.

Clinton nodded. "Jeffries, Eubanks, how are you?"

"Good," Jeffries replied. "I wish I weren't here, though, to be honest. I heard about that video you sent. Sounds nasty. What do you think's going on?"

"I don't know. Weird shit. Weird shit, and Justin ain't in the store, and that ain't like him."

"So, two missing persons?" Jeffries said. Catching a whiff of the foul odor, he scrunched up his nose. "Jesus Christ, it smells like a dead dog's asshole."

"Wait until you see what's back there."

Jeffries and Eubanks followed him to the rear of the building.

"You weren't kidding," Jeffries said, taking in the scene. "This is some weird shit."

They looked up to see a news helicopter flying overhead.

Eubanks finally spoke. "Where's the gun you found?"

"In them bushes." Clinton pointed.

Jeffries walked over and examined the gun in a drying pile of feces. He swallowed as if to keep his lunch down. The handle glinted through the shit. "Yeah, that's Pearl all right. Where is the sheriff?"

"The trail leads to that door. I'm guessing what we are looking for is inside that bathroom," Clinton replied.

"Are we sure he's even in there?"

"No, but either way we need to rule it out so someone needs to open that door so we can get this over with and I'm not doing it," Clinton said.

"Good idea," Jeffries said. "Eubanks, go ahead. We'll cover you."

Eubanks rolled his eyes as he edged near the door. When he got close, he looked back at Jeffries and Clinton, an uneasy expression on his face. They waved him on. As he grabbed the handle and turned it, the metal door burst violently outward. He flew backward ten feet and landed headfirst, his skull making a sickening crack as it hit the pavement. Eubanks's body crumpled to the ground, his head caved in on one side with a rapidly increasing pool of blood surrounding it.

A humanoid creature dripping with feces slid into view. It had arms but no legs and glided over the ground like a snail, leaving a brown train behind it. Jeffries gagged, startling the creature. Turning its attention to the officers, it let out a deep, guttural roar and emerged from the bathroom, rising to its full height. It towered over them.

The creature reached for Jeffries, chunks of vomit and diarrhea sliding off its limbs. Clinton had just enough time to register that it looked like a giant shit with arms and a head before Jeffries pulled his weapon and aimed. Clinton backed away and slipped under the tape. Jeffries fired three quick shots. The bullets made impact, splashing shit, then sank into its body. Jeffries aimed for the head and kept firing. The creature surged forward, reaching to grab him. He jumped back out of its grasp, passed under the tape, and fired again with the same result.

"Keep distracting it. I have a plan," Clinton said.

"It better be good. This thing is indestructible," Jeffries said, ducking as a fecal projectile sailed over his head and splattered on the ground.

"I'm going to try to blow it up."

"Blow it up?"

"I've got a couple of grenades in the truck," Clinton replied.

"Why the fuck do you have grenades?"

"I keep an arsenal in there. You never know when you're going to need to blow some shit up."

"Where the fuck? Never mind. I'll keep it distracted."

The creature closed in on Jeffries as Clinton turned and ran for his truck. Jeffries kept his aim on it. He opened fire one last time and was finally out of rounds. In a last desperate attempt to keep the shitpile occupied, he threw his gun at it. The weapon lodged in its side. The creature stopped, made a grunting noise, and extended one of its appendages forward. A hand began to take shape. The gun pushed out of the shit and slid into the newly formed hand.

"Clinton, it's got my gun," Jeffries yelled.

"The bullets would need shells!" Clinton yelled back.

"What is it doing then?"

Clinton heard a thunk and ducked, then glanced over the side of the truck at the shit monster standing there trying to aim the gun at Jeffries. The gun jerked and Clinton heard the same thunk sound and a pop. He saw a small projectile hit the side of the gas station and shatter, falling to the ground. The pieces were brown. The monster adjusted the weapon and tried again, getting closer this time. Jeffries continued backing away toward Clinton's truck, ducking every time it fired.

"Jeffries, you aren't going to believe this, but it's using bullets made out of shit."

One of the projectiles hit the pavement in front of Jeffries and shattered.

"Fuck me. I never thought I would die by a fucking turd nugget. Hurry up, man!" Jeffries bawled. "Its aim is getting better!"

Clinton reached the truck, raced around to the bed, opened the box in the back, and pulled out a grenade. He glanced over to where Jeffries was dodging the creature's bullets. They were getting closer. It stopped and hunched down like it was about to take a dump. Clinton laughed. A shit monster taking a shit was the most absurd thing he had ever seen.

This was his chance. It wasn't moving, and it was so big he was sure not to miss it. He pulled the pin, waited a few seconds, and threw it at the creature. A pile of bloody stool mixed with broken bones streamed out of its backside. The grenade stuck to the side of the shit monster. With a wet splat, the explosive sank into its body. Clinton ducked down behind the truck, peeking over the hood. As he began to wonder if he'd deployed a dud, the creature exploded. Chunky liquid shit and vomit flew everywhere, covering Jeffries head to toe in a cascade of excrement. A shower of feces reached Deputy Clinton's feet, and some rained down on his truck. He backed farther away as the downpour of dung continued its deluge.

When it was over, Clinton could taste the shit in his mouth. It looked like a bomb had gone off at the gas station. Jeffries, at ground zero, gently wiped the muck away from his eyes and then reached into his mouth and scraped shit out of it.

"Jeffries, are you okay?" Clinton called out through a gag

Jeffries shook his head *no*, then doubled over and vomited. "No, Clinton. I am not okay," he said when he was done. Jeffries's knees buckled, and he passed out and fell over backward, causing the brown slush below him to splash out to the sides.

Clinton laughed at the absurdity of the situation, not noticing the little white worm sliding through the diarrhea toward Jeffries. He reached out to click his radio. "Officer injured. Another down. Possible triple homicide."

The radio crackled.

"Ten-four."

He let go of the radio and carefully made his way to Jeffries. There was so much diarrhea in the parking lot that he kept sliding through it with each step.

"Jeffries!"

No answer.

He tried scooting his feet a little bit at a time to get closer. He wasn't about to fall into this nasty shit. It smelled like Richard Gere shit out a bunch of dead gerbils after an orgy, and he didn't want it all over him. Poor Jeffries was covered in it after the grenade blew up the shit monster. As he got closer, he heard a strange sound, like gas escaping from a balloon. Jeffries's abdomen swelled as the buttons on his uniform popped off.

"Jeffries!"

The downed cop was on his back. He groaned, opened his eyes, and farted as he tried to roll over on his side. Unable to stop himself, Clinton laughed.

"Not funny, Clinton," Jeffries groaned.

"You okay, man?"

"No. My stomach hurts, and it's getting worse. What is happening to me?"

"I don't know, man, but your stomach is swelling. You look like you're pregnant."

"Fuck! I feel like I have horrible gas, and need to drop a deuce. Oh, God!"

Jeffries rolled over on his back, and the rest of the buttons broke as his abdomen kept expanding. He screamed and spewed out a stream of slimy, brown shit. It didn't stop, and he frantically grabbed at his throat as he tried to roll over.

"Oh, fuck!" Clinton squawked.

Jeffries's eyes popped out one after the other as a steady stream of dookie flowed out of the sockets like chocolate soft-serve ice cream with corn sprinkles, and his ears leaked the same foul liquid. His pants ballooned and ripped at the seams, where more diarrhea flowed out. Clinton tried to move away faster but kept sliding in the muck. He scooted his feet a little at a time with his hands out to steady himself. As he neared the clean part of the parking lot, Jeffries's body burst, sending chunks of flesh and bone flying followed by another anal blast. Clinton tried to turn and run, but he was too close and it was too late. Shitty chunks of bone-shrapnel tore into his legs and abdomen, and he fell over on his back. An unholy rain of feces, blood, and flesh fell on him, covering him completely.

Clinton groaned and wiped his face as best as he could with his hands, then tried to stand. Finally, he was able to get to his feet and slung his arms around to get some of the shit off him. He recalled that on the side of the gas station, there was a hose connected to a water faucet, and he headed for it, no longer caring if he fell into the shit. A long, guttural moan came from behind him. He turned to look and another creature grew out of where Jeffries's body had exploded.

Its head and abdomen rose out of the gore, and it formed arms and began to scrape up the pieces of Jeffries's body and as much shit as it could get, absorbing it into itself and growing all the more. Clinton felt the hair rise on the back of his neck. As it took in the pieces of bone, the creature sprouted legs. It was building itself a skeleton, learning from its past mistakes and improving itself. Evolving. Clinton reached for his gun and unclasped it. Luckily, it was mostly free of shit. He clicked the safety off and looked up; the shit monster stood at its full height. Unlike its previous slug-like form, this time, the creature had legs.

It stared at Clinton, and he realized its eyes were made of balls of little white, slithering worms. His hands shook as he lifted the gun and screamed, hoping to scare it, while simultaneously firing. As they had before, the useless bullets splashed when they hit, and disappeared into the monster's body. The creature stood and studied him. It raised an appendage and pointed it at Clinton, holding it in the air as the shit began to form into a hand holding a gun. It was a real gun, Jeffries's gun. It tried to aim, and Clinton ducked and ran for his truck. There was nothing else to hide behind. The creature aimed and fired twice. The bullets missed and went into the forest beyond. Clinton kept running and had nearly reached the edge of the wood when the creature fired again, and the shit-bullet hit his left leg. He screamed in pain and fell, dropping his gun.

He looked back as he tried to get up. It was too late. The creature was upon him and reached out and grabbed his leg, lifting him in the air. As it absorbed him into its body, Clinton screamed and screamed and screamed.

I stopped typing and stood. All the noises above had ceased. Hopefully, everything was back to normal. Smiling, I waited for a message from Dakota, satisfied that I had created a nice, disgusting story, and it felt good to finish something. I didn't have to wait long.

It's done, and a deal is a deal. Everything is back to normal, as promised. I will take my leave of you. I got what I came for. Now, get to writing more stories and books like this, or I'll be back.

I sat and waited for more words to appear.

Nothing.

He must really be gone, I thought. I smiled and walked down the hall, climbed the ladder, and emerged from the bunker. Hunter was with his friends, putting the fishing gear away. I opened the sliding glass doors at the back of the house and walked into the living room to see my wife sitting on the couch watching the news, the same as earlier.

"Honey, listen to this. Something is going on at Phillips 66," she said.

I sat down and draped my arm around her. Her words sounded awfully familiar. I saw the same gas station and a sinking worry struck me that it was all happening again, until I looked at the screen and it was the same female reporter as before, but she was telling a story about a robbery. The camera captured a scruffy-looking man and woman in handcuffs being led out of the gas station by a police officer.

"How's your writing going?" Mary asked.

"It's going well. I've been working on a good story."

"What's it called?" she asked.

"Absorbed By Excrement."

"Ew."

Her disgust excited me. That was a good thing. People would know they were in for a ride when they saw it. Mary read all my books, but didn't like the sex or gore. Never once did she ask me to tone it down, though, probably because sex and violence sells like hotcakes, and she liked not working.

Hunter came in the back door, hollering, "Hey, we are going to the movies, okay?"

I turned my head. "That's fine. Just be careful."

"I know," he said, slamming the door.

"Don't slam the door!" I yelled, but he was gone.

We sat silently for a while, and I thought about when Mary was in the mood earlier. Maybe she would be again.

"You want to fool around again?" I asked.

"What do you mean again? Did you have a wet dream last night?" she asked.

Fuck. When everything returned to normal, Mary had forgotten everything that happened. It made sense. At least I remembered it. I sighed and kissed her cheek and grabbed her hand. We watched the news in silence. Later, a movie came on, and she cuddled next to me and fell asleep. As it got dark outside, I felt sleepy. I was ready to call it a day.

"I'm going to bed," I said, tapping Mary awake.

She sat up and yawned. "Okay, I'll be there in a bit."

I kissed her on the cheek again and got up from the couch. I went to our room, lay on the bed, and thought about the day's events. It had been a strange fucking day. I was glad it was over.

I fell asleep.

CHAPTER 8

I SLEPT HARDER THAN I usually do, and I must have slept weird because my back hurt. I got up, careful not to wake Mary while getting dressed, and went into the kitchen to make coffee. I loaded a cup into my Keurig. It was early. The sun was beginning to show itself through the blinds, and Hunter had come in sometime late the night before and was asleep. When the Keurig beeped I grabbed my cup and went outside to the bunker and headed straight to my desk. I had an idea for a new story and was eager to get started on something fresh.

Unfortunately *Absorbed by Excrement* was back on my laptop screen, and more words had been written. I didn't know whether to be pissed off or excited. Taking a sip of my coffee, I set the cup down. It needed time to cool off and I drummed my fingers on the desk while I debated if I wanted to read it, but I figured I would be forced to anyway, so I began:

Absorbed By Excrement
Part 5

A tall man reclined on a blanket under a thicket of pine trees. He held a lighter under a glass pipe while gently rolling it between his fingers, waiting for the crystals inside to melt. It wasn't long before he sucked on the end, rolling it the whole time so the liquid meth wouldn't burn. He stopped inhaling long enough to look down at the greasy blond hair of the woman whose mouth was bobbing up and down on his cock. He clutched her hair when the high hit, jammed her head down, and thrust his hips against her face. She gagged and pushed herself back.

"Jesus, Donnie. I almost threw up on your dick!"

The woman rubbed her head where he'd pulled her hair. He passed her the pipe and the lighter, and she snatched them from him.

"Sorry, Ellie. You know there's nuthin' better than getting head while blowing smoke."

"Just be careful next time, okay?" Ellie took a hit and handed the pipe back.

"Okay."

He watched her heat up the now-melted crystals and roll them back and forth. "Get over here and grab me by the pussy," she said, then inhaled.

He was more than happy to feel up her cooter. The meth made him so horny no sex act was off limits. Soon his face was between her legs when she exhaled, and he was happily lapping away as she grabbed his head with one hand and held it tight against her pussy and ground up and down while he stroked himself.

A third woman, loosely tied up against a tree nearby, finally spoke up. "Hey, I thought we were going to role-play," she said.

Ellie pushed him away. "Sorry Grace, I was so caught up I forgot you were there."

"So did I. Pass her the pipe," Donnie said.

"You guys better make it up to me," Grace said.

Ellie scooted next to Grace, untied her, and handed her the pipe, then Ellie put her hand between Grace's legs and began to rub her hairy pussy as she took a long hit and finally blew out the smoke.

"What was the plan again?" Donnie asked, looking at them both.

"Grace is going to play the kidnap victim. Then we threaten her if she doesn't do what we say, and make her give you head, then me, and then you fake rape her," Ellie said.

"That sounds awesome."

"Yeah, let's get it started, I'm ready to get fucked," Grace said.

Ellie turned to Grace and pointed a finger at her. "Babe, let's get her to suck us off while we smoke."

"Hell yeah. Then I want to knock the bitch up." Donnie rubbed his cock.

"I can't wait to see that."

Ellie grabbed the long, serrated knife from the top of her pile of clothes near the blanket. She stepped over to Grace, pointing the knife at her face. Grace flinched, playing the part. Ellie grew angry and grabbed a handful of Grace's hair and jerked her head back, tracing the weapon along her throat.

Grace moaned.

"You aren't supposed to be enjoying it," Ellie whispered.

"Make me hate it," Grace said and zipped up her lips.

Ellie got back into character. "Are you going to be good or am I going to have to cut your throat?"

"Please, don't hurt me! I'll do whatever you want! Please, I have a family!" Grace sobbed.

Ellie looked at Donnie stretched out on the blanket. He watched her and stroked himself.

"You like this baby?" she asked.

She lowered the knife and traced it around one of Grace's breasts, then the nipple, and back to the neck.

"Make that bitch play with herself while you run the knife over her," he said.

"You heard him," Ellie screamed at Grace.

Ellie's hand shook as she moved her hand down toward her crotch. Tears streamed down her face and dripped onto her chest. Ellie pressed the knife tight against Grace's neck.

"Get that hand on that pussy and rub it," she yelled.

Grace did as she was told and reached between her legs and rubbed herself. Donnie watched, and his hand pumped his cock faster.

"You gonna cum, baby? You wanted to fuck her too. Don't shoot yet."

He grunted in reply and kept going, watching Grace masturbate. She was a good find on Hinge, and tonight was their first time with her. Donnie couldn't stop jerking his gherkin long enough to get up and go fuck her. Ellie continued to slide the knife across Grace's throat and back while she masturbated. She was getting loud now, and it nearly sent Donnie over the edge.

A loud, booming roar echoed throughout the forest. Ellie jumped in fright, accidentally slicing open Grace's throat. Warm arterial spray spurted all over her chest and dripped down her breasts. It looked like a tank top made from blood. The gore kept squirting out of the wound in Grace's neck. She slumped backward. Red dripped over her tits, her stomach, and her hand that still had a finger inside her pussy. The squirting stopped, and it continued to pour out onto her chest.

"Oh my god!" Ellie screamed.

"Fuck yeah!" Donnie grunted.

He dropped to his knees, jerking his cock over Grace's body, and his cum shot on her tits.

"Donnie! What the fuck? She's fucking dead! We need to get the fuck out of here!"

"Oh fuck! I got carried away. The meth had me in a frenzy."

She kicked him and dropped the knife. "Dumbass, now they'll have your DNA."

"I'll clean it up."

"Didn't you hear that noise? There's a bear out here somewhere. Get dressed. Grab the meth and the pipe. We need to leave now. Go to Mexico or something, If we get caught, it's lethal injection for sure!"

"Hot as it was, you're the one that slit her throat."

"Donnie, you idiot, that's the meth talking, and it's your jizz on her corpse."

"Fuck," he said.

They struggled to find their clothes and dress. Ellie got done first and looked for her purse. She hadn't meant to kill Grace but her hands still shook. Donnie was putting his shirt on, when another roar echoed around them, followed by a person screaming, and a single gunshot.

"Jesus, Donnie, what the fuck was that?" Ellie asked, frantically searching for her purse.

Donnie tapped her on the shoulder, holding the knock-off Prada bag in his hand. "That sounded close, and big."

"Oh God, what is that smell?"

"Jesus, someone is fertilizing their crops."

"We need to think. We are in real trouble here!"

He grabbed her around the hip, pulled her in, and kissed her. "You gotta admit that it was hot."

She smiled at him. "Yeah, it was. Okay, let's get out of here." She pushed him away.

Ellie followed Donnie through the woods. They headed for his car parked at the Phillips 66. She hadn't wanted to fuck in the woods, but considering the circumstances, she was glad they did. Hopefully, it would be a while before anyone found Grace's body. She felt she should feel worse about killing her friend, but she didn't; it turned her on. It was probably the meth making her feel that way.

"Donnie, do you feel bad about Grace?"

He stopped to look at her and smiled. "I haven't cum that hard in a long time, so no, not really."

"That makes me feel better. I thought maybe it was the meth making me feel that way, but I guess I just liked it."

"Then we'll do it again. We better get going, all this talk is making my dick hard."

He ran his hand over her ass and leaned in for a kiss. They flinched away, hearing a gunshot, followed by another. A bullet flew by their heads and lodged into a tree.

They ran as fast as they could. She went first, moving tree limbs out of the way that would bounce back, hitting Donnie.

"Dammit, babe, be careful!"

Ellie didn't reply. She kept running until they burst out of the foliage. They stopped at the strange scene in a parking lot before them. The smell was overwhelming, like getting in an elevator after someone ripped a silent but deadly ass blaster.

Ellie leaned over and threw up.

Most of the lot was covered in maggot-infested shit with worms crawling around all over and inside it. Flies buzzed, landed on it and then flew back up into the air. Standing in the middle was a gigantic pile of walking ass vomit mixed with blood and bones. It looked like a sewer main blasted all over some poor bastard and he was awkwardly trying to figure out how to walk with all the extra weight. They watched as chunks of feces fell off and splattered onto the asphalt and then were absorbed into its body through its feet. Dangling from its abdomen was the top half of a man struggling to get free as he sank into it. He flailed back and forth, trying to wiggle himself out, but it was too strong. Soon, he was up to his shoulders.

"Oh god, that man is being sucked into the turd!" Donnie said.

"Shut up, Donnie. It'll hear you," Ellie whispered.

The police officer noticed them. "Help me!" His scream echoed throughout the forest. He made a gurgling sound as he drowned in diarrhea, then his head disappeared into the creature.

"How much meth did we smoke?" Donnie asked.

"I don't know, shit! Hold on. I put the pipe in my purse."

"Forget it. We gotta go or we are gonna die, babe."

They ran to their vehicle, an old, beat-up, gray Chevy Blazer. Getting in, Donnie searched for the keys, usually stashed in the ashtray but they weren't there. He looked around the car, in the console, on the floor, then searched his pockets.

"Donnie," Ellie whispered.

He continued looking for the keys.

"Donnie!" she screeched.

He turned his head. The monster's hand had grown to twice the size of their car and was hurtling toward them. It grabbed the vehicle and lifted it. Donnie opened the door and jumped. He screamed all the way down, and his body splattered onto the parking lot. Terrified, Ellie couldn't move. The creature squeezed, popping the car like a pimple, and Ellie burst like a blister, her body squirting out through the cracks of the crushed Chevy. The monster dropped the car and walked into the forest toward the lake.

"Fucking hilarious, right?" a voice said from behind me. I jumped out of my chair.

I turned to face the most disgusting thing I had ever seen. A naked man, or creature, stood behind me. Its skin was red with hints of blue, like a giant bruise filled with cuts, scabs, and pus-filled sores all over his body. Its face had more piercings than I thought possible. Two small horns protruded from its forehead, and its cock was at least seven inches long with rings from the tip down to the balls on the underside, with a bigger ring on the head. It had talons for toenails.

"Oops," it said in a deep voice.

I watched its body twitch and shake, transforming and changing colors. When it settled down, a man stood there in its place. It was Dakota, as I remembered him from when he was terrorizing my family.

"My time here is almost done, and I wanted to talk to you in person," Dakota said.

"You scared the shit out of me, asshole," I admonished.

Dakota examined the bunker like he had never seen it before.

"The part of the story you wrote isn't happening in real life somewhere, is it? I mean, the shit monster isn't coming to life again?" I asked.

"Why? Do you want it to?"

"No. Once was enough." My dick was half hard from reading the story.

"Looks like you enjoyed the sex scenes. If you want, I can make it where Mary is more receptive to you," he said.

"What are you talking about?"

"You've seen what I can do. I can make Mary want to fuck all the time, and her pussy is always wet. I know you want it. I watch you jerk off all the time."

"Gross, but I'm listening."

"You'll never jerk off again. Your wife would be your own real-life fuck doll. And if you decide you don't like it, I can always change her back to how she is now."

"What's the catch?"

"No catch. I just want you to get what you deserve."

It would be like a dream come true. As much pussy as I wanted. It was an easy decision. "All right, as long as nothing bad happens, let's do it."

"It's done." He smiled.

The door to the bunker clanged open. Mary came down the ladder. Still in her robe, she walked with confidence.

"Who is your friend?" She looked the visitor up and down. Her eyes locked on his penis and she licked her lips, then looked up at his face. "Jesus, is that Dakota Blackwell?"

"Yeah," I said.

"Even better looking than I remember."

She sat on the bed and spread her legs and ran her hands all over her body. Dakota was hard as a rock. This might turn into a threesome, something I've tried to get her into for years.

"Damn, you're sexy. Why don't you come over here and fuck me," she said to him.

"You sure about this?" Dakota asked me.

"Hell yeah, fuck her," I said.

I was so excited this was about to happen. He climbed on the bed and got between Mary's legs.

"He will like it," she said to Dakota, then to me, "won't you honey? You've always wanted to watch me get fucked. You fucking pervert."

It was true. I watched as she wrapped her legs around him. He slid his cock into her pussy and thrust in and out slowly a few times, then stopped and held still.

"Why did you stop? Fuck me!" Mary cried.

He was as still as a dog drooling at its master's cheeseburger.

"Dakota?" I asked.

He made a loud guttural moan, and his body twitched, and then violently shook. His skin turned blue, balls deep in Mary, and he changed into his demonic form. She screamed and tried pushing him away. He held her down with one hand and pumped in and out of her. The rings lining his cock had an immediate effect. Soon she moaned, relaxed, and began to enjoy it. I was finally getting to watch her fuck another person. Well, a monster, my wife was fucking a demonic monster. I unzipped my pants and pulled out my dong.

She waved me over, and I climbed up on the bed on my knees and scooted over by her face. She leaned her head forward to take my dick into her mouth as Dakota clenched up his face and started to cum. So did Mary. She screamed, "Oh, God!" and passed out.

Dakota laughed and climbed off her. He sat on the desk chair while I got on top of her for sloppy seconds.

"It's almost like I'm fucking a corpse," I said, savoring the feeling as I slid into her.

I slowly pumped in and out a few times. She was out cold. I kept going.

"You want to feel the real thing?" Dakota asked.

"What?"

"I said, do you want to feel the real thing? You know, fuck a corpse?"

I stopped thrusting and looked at him. He handed me a knife. "Slit her throat while you fuck her, and you'll really be fucking a corpse."

"What? Why would I do that?"

"I know you want to. I can see it in your mind's eye. You're thinking about it right now. Tell me you don't want to fuck Mary while she's dead. Besides, I can bring her back."

Deep down, I knew I would do it. It was like the ultimate sexual experience, and I have always wanted to try it, though I've never said it out loud. The very thought was making me want to cum.

"Yeah, I kinda do," I whispered and began thrusting.

Plus, like he said, he could always bring Mary back. What harm would it do? I ran the knife over her neck, testing how it felt.

"Do it. You know you want to," Dakota whispered.

The steel looked good against her flesh. Anticipation was killing me. I couldn't wait anymore. I sliced deep into her neck and ran the blade clear across it. The arterial spray shot all over me and onto her chest, and I lowered my head to take a bloody nipple into my mouth. I rolled around it with my tongue. The salty, metallic taste almost sent me over the edge. I slowed, so I wouldn't cum. I glanced over at Dakota, who was violently masturbating, and I switched my attention to the other nipple. As I savored the taste of her warm blood, her pussy twitched and clamped down on my cock. It was too much for me to handle. I started cumming. I had never felt anything so wonderful. I was in another world as I added my load to her already full pussy.

The bunker shook violently. I fell against Mary's body. The quaking worsened. Dakota's eyes glowed red, much like the shit monster in the story, and he grinned from ear to ear.

"What is happening?" I asked.

"Looks like you graduated," he replied.

"Bring Mary back now—you promised."

"No time for that." His body convulsed.

The floor split apart below the bed. A fissure formed down the hallway. The rumbling continued, and the crack rapidly expanded, followed by a sound like a freight train barreling down a track, or an incoming tornado.

"What do you mean, graduated?" I yelled.

"The master is pleased, and we will burn in the eternal fire together!"

The fissure kept growing. I was sweating. The heat intensified. "I thought you were going to bring Mary back! What about the story and corrupting the souls!"

"It's too late! The things you have done are enough to fulfill his needs. Look, he comes," Dakota said with glee.

The crack in the floor opened into a deep, dark chasm. Dakota stood at the edge and beckoned for me to join him. "Come," he said. "We will be together for eternity. It's what I wanted all along. I love you, Joshua."

"You planned this?"

"I want us to be together forever. Don't you want the same?" he asked with pleading eyes.

"This isn't what I want! I want my wife back! I want to live!" I screamed.

Out of the corner of my eye, I saw an orange glow. A giant tendril shot out of the chasm and wrapped around my abdomen. I screamed, and another wrapped around my legs. The pain was unbearable, like hundreds of little flames burning my skin.

"We will be together for eternity!" Dakota said triumphantly and jumped into the chasm.

I realized I had made a terrible mistake. Dakota had tricked me into killing Mary. He was still the same obsessive stalker, even in death. Now my wife was dead, and I was on my way to hell, and I would have to spend eternity there with that asshole.

A third tendril wrapped around my face, and I screamed in agony. The skin underneath began to melt. I had never felt pain like it. The tendrils lifted me off the bed and pulled me down into the chasm as my skin caught fire and began to burn. I could hear it sizzling.

The chasm closed, and everything returned to how it was. Mary's body was gone, and the blood had disappeared. A clang sounded from above, followed by footsteps down the ladder.

"Mom, Dad, I'm home!" Hunter called out.

He walked into the bedroom and looked around. No one was there. The laptop beeped, catching his attention, and writing appeared on the screen. It kept coming for several minutes. Hunter walked over to the desk and sat down and read the title aloud: "*Absorbed By Excrement*, by Josh Meyers and Dakota Blackwell."

AFTERWORD

I FOUND THIS MANUSCRIPT on a laptop in my father's bunker. For anyone out there seeing this: Thank you for reading his only book. His delusions of grandeur and fame were eclipsed by his insanity, which grew worse toward the end, and I am glad to have published this sick, disgusting volume so that I may use it to keep his memory alive. Enjoy.

– *Hunter Meyers*

ABOUT THE AUTHOR

MICHAEL ERROL SWAIM IS a horror and fantasy author who survived a liver and kidney transplant in 2019. His work has appeared in anthologies from The Horror Zine, Dark Moon Rising Publications, Wicked Shadow Press, Hellbound books, Carnage House, and more. His first published horror story, "The Blood," appeared in Issue 3 of the Carnage House 'zine, and shortly thereafter he was invited to join the Carnage House editorial staff. He lives in Northeast Oklahoma with his wife Mandy, his kids, and Wolfgirl the cat. *Absorbed By Excrement* is his first novella.